Feminist Fables for the
Twenty-First Century

Feminist Fables for the Twenty-First Century

The F Word Project

MAUREEN BURDOCK

Foreword by Trina Robbins

McFarland & Company, Inc., Publishers
Jefferson, North Carolina

Each tale was written and illustrated by
Maureen Burdock except for "Halima's Story,"
which was written by Halima Mohammed Abdel Rahman.

Additional Credits, by Story
Marta & the Missing
Gabriel de Pablo: Spanish translation / Fransicso Arce: Introduction
Mona & the Little Smile
Sarah Lightman: Introduction
Maisa & the Most Daring Muslim Women
Halima Mohammed Abdel Rahman: Arabic translation / Rubina Cohen: Introduction
Mumbi & the Long Run
David Opiyo: Swahili translation / Helen Concannon: Introduction /
Norah Sirma and Ester Korir: Afterword
Halima's Story
Written by Halima Mohammed Abdel Rahman

LIBRARY OF CONGRESS CATALOGUING-IN-PUBLICATION DATA

Feminist fables for the twenty-first century : the F Word Project / Maureen Burdock.
p.   cm.
Includes bibliographical references and index.

ISBN 978-0-7864-7423-3 (softcover : acid free paper) ∞
ISBN 978-1-4766-1294-2 (ebook)

1. Feminists—Comic books, strips, etc.   2. Feminism—Comic books, strips, etc.
3. Violence against women—Prevention—Comic books, strips, etc.   4. Child abuse—
Prevention—Comic books, strips, etc.   5. Women heroes—Comic books, strips, etc.
6. Graphic novels.   I. Burdock, Maureen, 1970– artist, compiler.   II. Robbins, Trina,
writer of foreword.   III. Lightman, Sarah, 1975– writer of introduction.   IV. De Pablo,
Gabriel, translator.   V. Arce, Francisco, writer of introduction.   VI. Rahman, Halima
Mohammed Sbdel, translator, author.   VII. Cohen, Rubina, writer of introduction.
VIII. Opiyo, David, translator.   IX. Concannon, Helen, writer of introduction.
X. Sirma, Norah, writer of afterword.   XI. Korir, Ester,
writer of afterword.   XII. Title: F Word Project.

PN6720.F46 2015   741.5'9—dc23   2015018552

BRITISH LIBRARY CATALOGUING DATA ARE AVAILABLE

Cover illustrations by Maureen Burdock

Printed in the United States of America

McFarland & Company, Inc., Publishers
Box 611, Jefferson, North Carolina 28640
www.mcfarlandpub.com

To those feminists who come after me
and courageously continue the work, and
with gratitude to all those who came before.

Acknowledgments

Thanks to the many folks who have supported and encouraged this project since its conception. I especially want to acknowledge 656 Comics and Palabras de Arena in Ciudad Juarez, Mexico. You are the ones who inspired me to start this project, and the example you set as passionate, humanist, feminist men and women has affected all of the fables in this collection.

Thank you to my translators: Gabriel de Pablo (Marta & the Missing), Halima Mohammed Abdel Rahman (Maisa & the Most Daring Muslim Women), and David Opiyo Ossome (Mumbi & the Long Run). Thanks also to my mother, Ingrid Claussner, for editing my translation of Mona & the Little Smile.

Thanks to Judy Chicago for encouraging me to complete this series of feminist fables and to the galleries and gallerists who have shown this work.

Rubina Cohen, thank you for sharing your stories with me, which found their way into Maisa & the Most Daring Muslim Women.

Many thanks to Jon Woo and the athletes of Camp Marafiki in Santa Fe, New Mexico. Not only did running with you make Mumbi and her comrades come alive in the fourth fable, but the experience gave me a deeper understanding of the meaning of community across cultures based on shared passion.

Thanks to Helen Concannon and the Friends of Londiani for sharing your knowledge with me, and to Sally Blakemore for your encouragement and for sharing your resources about FGM/C.

Halima Mohammed Abdel Rahman, your honest and open correspondences with me over the last few years have moved me deeply and made me realize the importance of finishing this project. You are truly a sister.

Contents

Author's Note

Feminism isn't dead. It can't be, because too many of us feminists are very much alive and working hard for gender equality. I created this series of feminist fables to exhibit how different forms of violence against women's bodies in distinct cultures around the world are linked. NO forms of gender-based violence should be condoned. I hope that this collection gives courage to individual women, and that it will be used as a tool to create feminist solidarity.

Feminism is a struggle for gender equality that has been carried out over centuries and across cultures. It is a struggle for a partnership-based society that is radically different from the binaristic Judeo-Christian-Islamic mythos of master-servant/shepherd-sheep/Lord-disciple/etc. relationships. We will no longer need feminism when:

1) We stop feminizing or masculinizing human characteristics.
2) There is no more bride burning, female genital mutilation, rape, honor killing, gay-bashing, or any other form of violence, physical or psychological, committed towards people because they display certain gender characteristics or because they refuse or fail to display "correct" gender markers.
3) Women earn the same as men.
4) The first thing said upon getting an ultrasound or giving birth is not "It's a girl" or "It's a boy."
5) And here's the real litmus test: When men—even those in positions of power—can feel free to wear dresses and skirts in public without being ridiculed.

Oh, that F Word!
A Foreword by Trina Robbins

These are very exciting times for women cartoonists. There are more women drawing comics today than ever before, and what they are drawing are graphic novels featuring real and fictional stories, sometimes funny, sometimes sad, sometimes scary, and very often empowering.

But many people still think comics are only about superheroes. And many people know only one kind of superhero: the muscular man in his cape and brightly colored costume; stern, angry, using his fists of steel to fight criminals, super-villains, monsters from outer space. In *Feminist Fables for the Twenty-First Century* Maureen Burdock introduces us to a different kind of superhero, and first of all, she's a girl. She doesn't wear capes, but sometimes, like marathon runner Mumbi in "Mumbi & the Long Run," she can fly. Sometimes, like Marta, the karate instructor in "Marta & the Missing," she even has fists of steel. Sometimes her superpowers lie in the magic of her art, always in her hard work, her determination, and her strong sense of justice. And in case you didn't get that they are superheroes, Mona, in "Mona & the Little Smile," even wears Wonder Woman underoos and ties around her head a starry scarf like Wonder Woman's tiara. And instead of monsters from outer space, what these brave girls fight are real evils: femicide, rape, incest, genital mutilation, domestic violence, so-called "honor killings."

With some very beautiful and some very frightening images, Maureen Burdock introduces us to female superheroes from countries all over the world. Most of these heroines are fictional though their stories are based on reality, but "Halima's Story" is true and documents the advocacy of a very real-life heroine. Their stories are told in English, and in the language of their own people.

A word about Maureen Burdock's art: sometimes it takes on the look of the folk art of the country she's writing about. This is especially true in "Maisa & the Most Daring Muslim Women," where she draws Maisa riding on the mythical bird-creature, the Simurgh, or where she shows us Maisa in her coffin underground, surrounded by strange godlike monster faces. My favorite art is in "Mumbi & the Long Run." I like the way Maureen conveys the freedom that Mumbi feels as she runs, almost flying like the superhero she is.

Maureen is somewhat of a superhero herself. She founded the San Francisco branch of Laydeez Do Comics, an international group of women cartoonists and woman-friendly men who meet in London, Chicago, and San Francisco to share ideas and to support each other's work. And if you think Laydeez Do Comics is a good idea, and that you could use a group like that, of women cartoonists meeting for idea sharing and support, in your own home town of Philly, St. Paul, Indianapolis, Denver, then take a page from Maureen's book and just DIY. To paraphrase Arlo Guthrie in "Alice's Restaurant," if three people do it, folks may think it's an organization, but if fifty people do it, folks may think it's a MOVEMENT. Let's start a movement!

So what is this F word, and why does it inspire hope in the hearts and minds of some and fear in the hearts of others? And what is there to be afraid of, anyway? Sure, the F word stands for Feminism, but for so much more. It stands for Fantastic, Formidable, Fabulous, and Feisty. It stands for Fierce, Fiery, Fervent, and Forceful. And it stands for Freedom, Fairness, Friendship, and the Future.

Award-winning herstorian and writer Trina Robbins has been writing books, comics, and graphic novels for more than 40 years. Her 2009 book, *The Brinkley Girls: The Best of Nell Brinkley's Cartoons from 1913–1940* (Fantagraphics), and her 2011 book, *Tarpe Mills and Miss Fury*, were nominated for Eisner awards and Harvey awards. Her all-ages graphic novel, *Chicagoland Detective Agency: The Drained Brains Caper*, first in a 6-book series, was a Junior Library Guild Selection. Her graphic novel, *Lily Renee: Escape Artist*, was awarded a gold medal from Moonbeam Chidren's Books and a silver medal from Sydney Taylor Jewish Library Awards. Her most recent book is *Pretty in Ink*, a definitive history of women cartoonists. In 2013, Trina was voted into the Will Eisner Comic Book Hall of Fame.

Marta & the Missing

Marta y Las Desaparecidas

Spanish Translation by Gabriel de Pablo

Introduction

In this desert city so eager for water and letters, so distant from everything yet so close to death, Ciudad Juarez is plagued by social problems. It is difficult to take a subject that is so debilitating to the soul of a Juarense as the femicides and leave us with a message of hope, but *Marta & the Missing* accomplishes that and more. I would like to give thanks to Maureen for taking the time and dedication to create this great graphic narrative, for it is a great example of commitment for women's rights and for a life without violence. Two strong women filled with convictions like Marta and Maureen really set examples to follow.

—Francisco Arce, director of Mecenas Galeria Studio
and writer of 656 Comics, Ciudad Juarez, Mexico

This story is dedicated, with deep feeling and respect, to all of those women lost and those who lost them. May this story inspire all those who stand together to stop violence against women around the world.

Dedico este libro, con sentimiento y profundo respeto, a todas esas mujeres desaparecidas y a sus familias. Ojalá esta historia sirva de inspiración a todas aquellas personas que luchan para frenar la violencia contra las mujeres en el mundo.

The women and girls in this story are modeled after actual women who were murdered in Ciudad Juarez, Mexico.

Los dibujos que aparecen en este libro fueron sacados de fotografías de mujeres y niñas reales que fueron asesinadas en Ciudad Juarez, Chihuahua, México.

Alma Margarita

Gloria

Hilda Johana

Edith

6

8

To be completely honest, I've never been to Mexico.
Para ser completamente honesta, nunca he estado en México.

But I met Marta, a woman from Juarez. I'll tell you how I met her later on. I don't remember what she does during the day. She might be a teacher, a maquiladora or a hair dresser.

Un día conocí a Marta, una mujer de Cd. Juarez. No recuerdo a qué se dedica Marta durante el día. Tal vez sea maestra, maquiladora o a lo mejor estilista. Pero por las tardes, ella hace lo que realmente le apasiona, ¡Ser instructora de Karate!

In the evenings Marta really comes alive as a Karate instructor.
Pero, mejor les cuento más adelante como la conocí.

10

After class, she walks home through the streets of the city with Pepito, her sidekick.

Después de clase, se regresa a casa caminando seguida de su canchanchán, el fiel y noble Pepito.

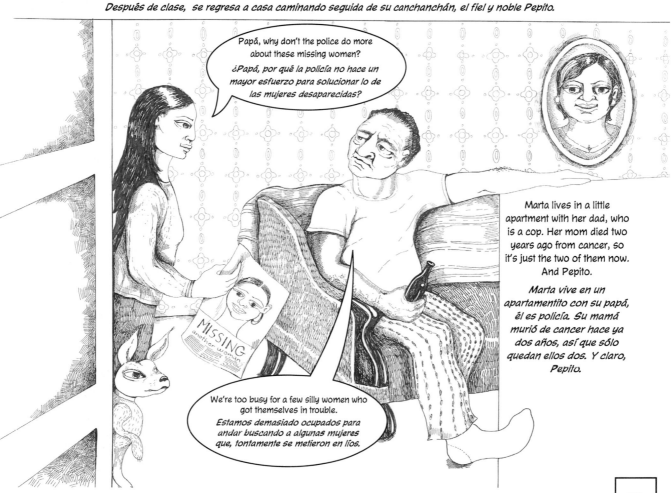

Papá, why don't the police do more about these missing women?

¿Papá, por qué la policía no hace un mayor esfuerzo para solucionar lo de las mujeres desaparecidas?

Marta lives in a little apartment with her dad, who is a cop. Her mom died two years ago from cancer, so it's just the two of them now. And Pepito.

Marta vive en un apartamentito con su papá, él es policía. Su mamá murió de cancer hace ya dos años, así que sólo quedan ellos dos. Y claro, Pepito.

We're too busy for a few silly women who got themselves in trouble.

Estamos demasiado ocupados para andar buscando a algunas mujeres que, tontamente se metieron en líos.

11

At night, a very mysterious woman awakens Marta and leads her into the dark city.

En la noche una misteriosa mujer despierta a Marta y la conduce por la oscuridad de la ciudad.

14

. . . Next morning, Marta is very sleepy, so she goes out to buy coffee.
. . . A la mañana siguiente, aún con sueño, Marta sale por un cafecito.

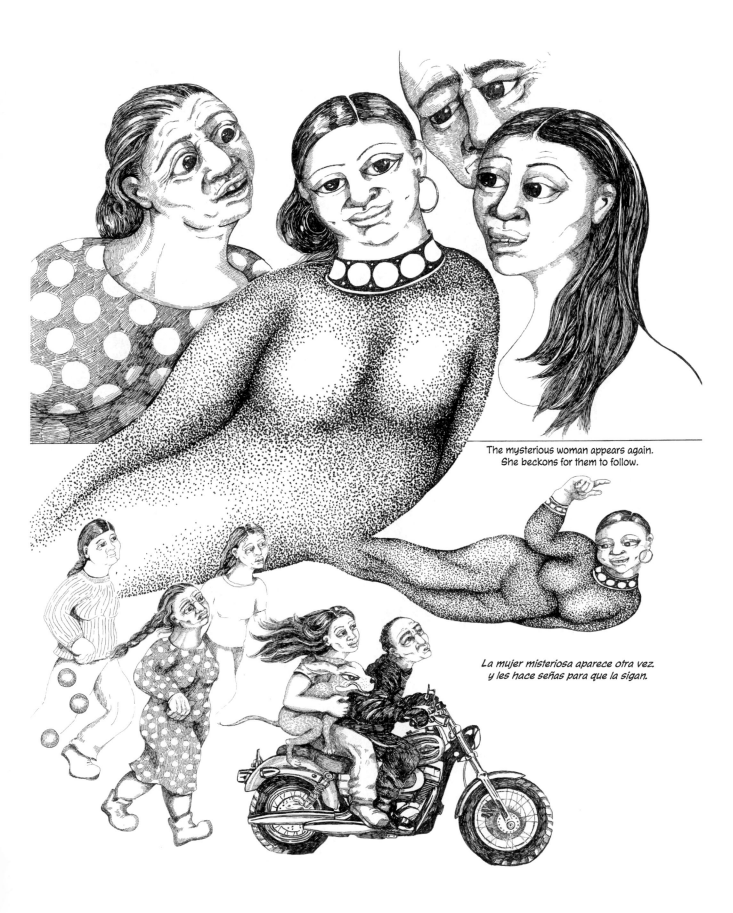

The mysterious woman appears again.
She beckons for them to follow.

*La mujer misteriosa aparece otra vez.
y les hace señas para que la sigan.*

17

19

The pursuit is on. People suddenly appear from all directions, chasing down the car with the little boy's scared sister.

The people of Juarez have had enough!

Y así comienza la persecución, empieza a aparecer gente por todos lados, todos persiguiendo al auto de los secuestradores.

La gente de Juarez yá está hasta la madre de los secuestros.

21

Soon, hordes of people surround the perpetrators.

En minutos, los criminales se vieron completamente rodeados.

I promised I'd tell you how I met Marta. I don't remember what she does during the day.
She might be a teacher, a maquiladora or a hair dresser.
But I met her at night, in my dreams.

No recuerdo que hace Marta durante el da. Tal vez sea maestra, maquiladora o estilista.
Pero prometí decirles cómo conocí a Marta ¿Quieres saber?
La conocí una noche, en mis suñeos.

Please come with us, quickly!
Women all over the world need your help.

Porfavor, ¡únete ahora!
Son muchas las mujeres que necesitan de nuestra ayuda!

Érika

Fabiola

Liliana

Maria Elena

Ana Lidia

... y muchas, muchas más.

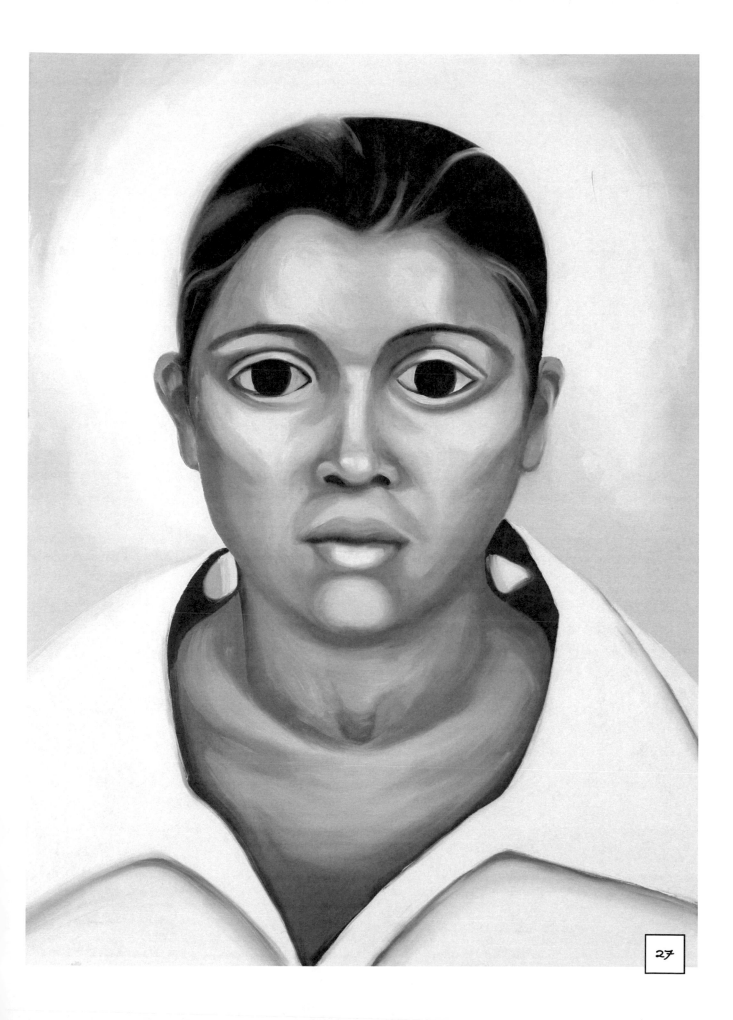

27

Mona & the Little Smile

Mona & Das Leise Lächeln

For all the children who got their smiles back by
squatting on the earth and putting their minds together—
and for all those who will.

*Für alle Kinder die ihr Lächeln wiederfanden in dem sie sich auf
den Erdboden hockten und die Köpfchen zusasmmensteckten—
und für die, die das noch tun werden.*

Introduction
Sarah Lightman

It may seem that comics are a surprising format for Maureen Burdock's "Mona & the Little Smile," a story of sexual abuse, but autobiographical comics have been a venue for coming to terms with personal atrocities for many decades. In terms of content and audience, Art Spiegelman's Holocaust memoirs *Maus* (1986–1991), were a watershed for the art form. However, I would like to suggest that Burdock's "Mona & the Little Smile" has older roots, first appearing in the 1970s and continuing to flourish into the present, with women illustrating their lives, their stories—*herstories*. Through the brave and intimate sharing of personal stories of domestic violence, abuse and personal tragedy, grief and rage dissipate with repeated exposure to light and air and validation of shared experience.

In her graphic memoir *Love That Bunch*, Aline Kominsky-Crumb includes a distressing rape encounter told with a dispassionate tone and depicts her father forcing himself on her mother. And the title of Diane Noomin's seminal work, *Baby Talk: A Tale of Four Miscarriages,* reveals her no longer private tragedies.

These life stories happened in internalized spaces: miscarriages inside the woman's body, sexual and spousal abuse within the family, in the family home. Comics, in their constructed and contained world of panels and borders, offer a space both closed and open to the public. These everyday stories that have previously been silenced, or kept hidden in cultures of silence, find a voice and a space on the comics page.

In this telling of a harrowing story of child sexual abuse the pages are insistent, like recurring nightmares, recreating the trauma, yet in doing so also catalyzing transformation. Clara Jo Stember, an art therapist who was a pioneer in helping sexually abused children, noted: "Since the trauma of sexual abuse is primarily psychological, artwork can provide a vehicle for bringing even deeply repressed trauma to the surface."

Many pages of "Mona & the Little Smile" are just images, and it is possible to read the story without words. Additionally, the minimal text appears in English and German indicating how her experience, and the vulnerability of children, is not limited to one culture. Mona later uses her drawings to save children from around the world: language becomes irrelevant as the drawings are universally understood.

Also depicted are how the traumatic events resulted in Mona's need to create an alternative self. Other symptoms of dissociation are reflected in the comic as the narrative develops from reality into fantasy, and as the illustrations change from tightly rendered pen drawings to colorful whimsical paintings.

Mona is shown making "magical drawings" and sending them "to children in danger." These drawings save the children, and the victims decide to punish the perpetrators by reduction: "Collectively they decide that all child molesters would be turned into organic, harmless life forms ... mushrooms." Mona is drawn squatting near the mushrooms: "She felt wonderful, the mushrooms were perfectly silly." The beginning and end of "Mona & the Little Smile" are filled with these mushrooms, richly painted, in earthy colors. These pages of paintings have no words; those guilty of the crimes of abuse are silenced and disempowered and the children, whose stories have now been shared, and thus validated, can begin to heal.

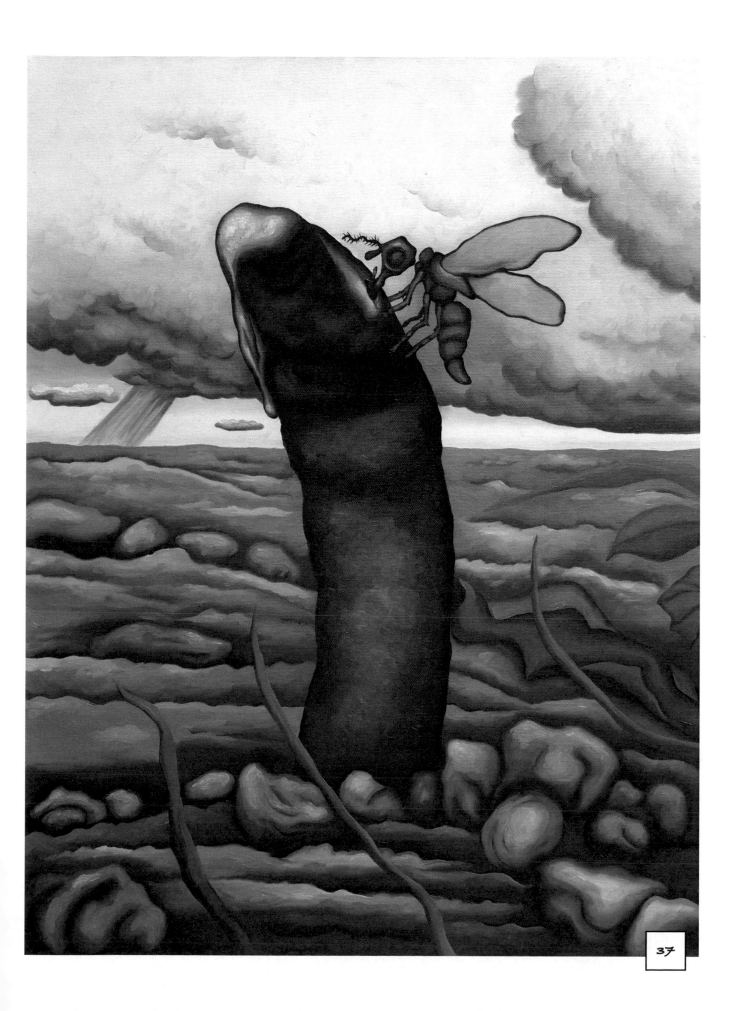

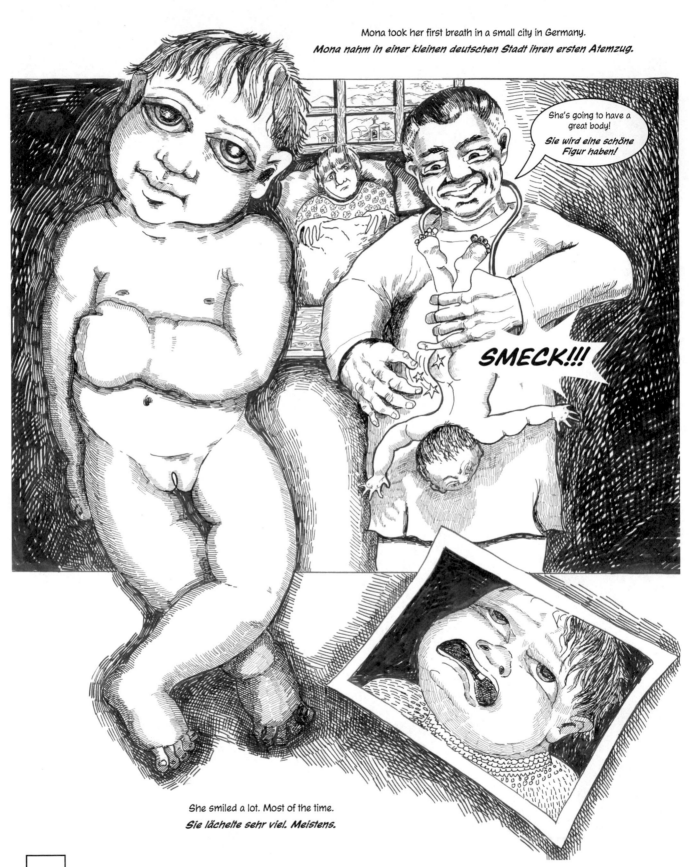

Mona took her first breath in a small city in Germany.
Mona nahm in einer kleinen deutschen Stadt ihren ersten Atemzug.

She smiled a lot. Most of the time.
Sie lächelte sehr viel. Meistens.

She grew up like a normal little German girl.

Sie wurde ganz normal als kleines deutsches Mädchen erzogen.

Hey look, let's pretend you have breasts!

Schau mal was für einen schönen Busen du hast!

grapefruit skins from breakfast

Pampelmusenschalen vom Frühstück

Or did she? What was normal, really?

wurde sie das wirklich? Was heisst normal?

thud

dumb bitch

blöde kuh

sob

heul

I fell down the stairs.

Ich bin die Treppe runter gefallen.

41

Mona and her mother ran away to America. Mother went back to Germany to finalize the divorce.

Mona und ihre Mutter flüchteten nach Amerika. Mutter kehrte nach Deutschland zurück, um den Scheidungsprozess zu erledigen.

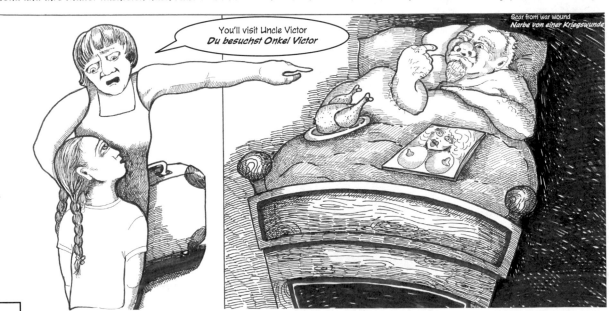

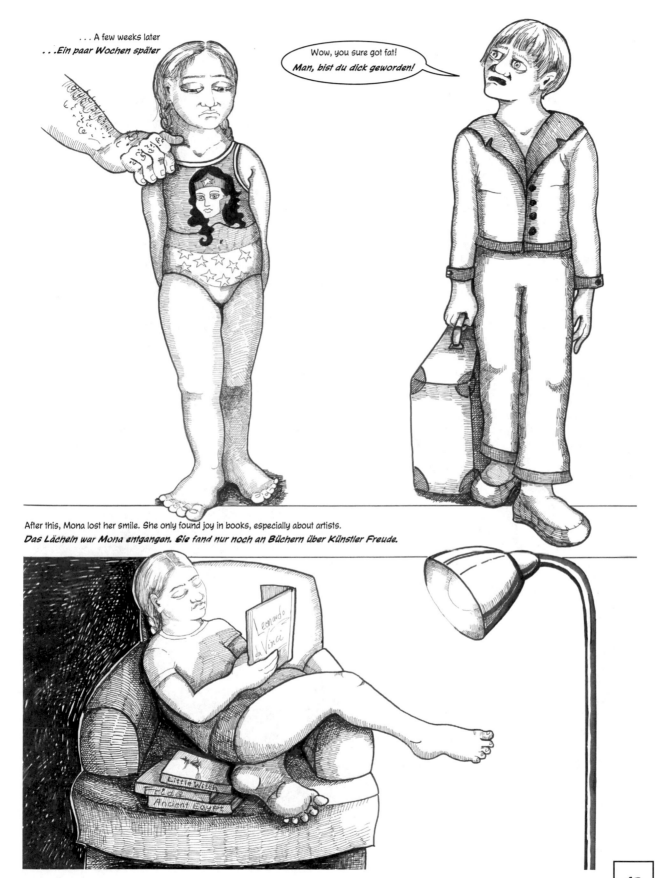

Mona saw that art can change things,
so she drew and drew until she changed herself.

Mona glaubte, dass Kunst alles umgestalten kann.
Sie malte und malte bis sie sich selbst umgewandelt hatte.

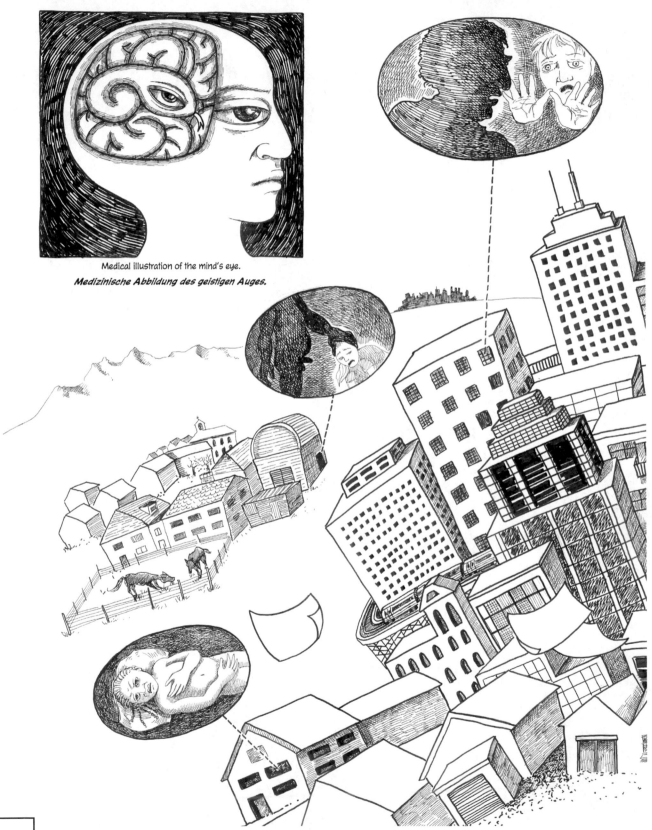

Medical illustration of the mind's eye.

Medizinische Abbildung des geistigen Auges.

In her mind's eye, Mona saw that many children like herself still needed to change, too.

So she made thousands of magical drawings and sent them to children in danger, who could use them to transform themselves into any shape they wanted.

In ihrem geistigen Auge sah Mona, dass viele Kinder, ihr selbst ähnlich, noch Umwandlung benötigten.

Also zeichnete sie tausende von Bildern, damit die Kinder in Gefahr sie zu unbegrenzten Verwandlungmöglichkeiten einsetzen könnten.

47

Upon reaching the innocent ones, the drawings caused awesome calamity!

Als die Zeichnungen die Kleinen erreichten, stellten sie alles total auf den Kopf!

49

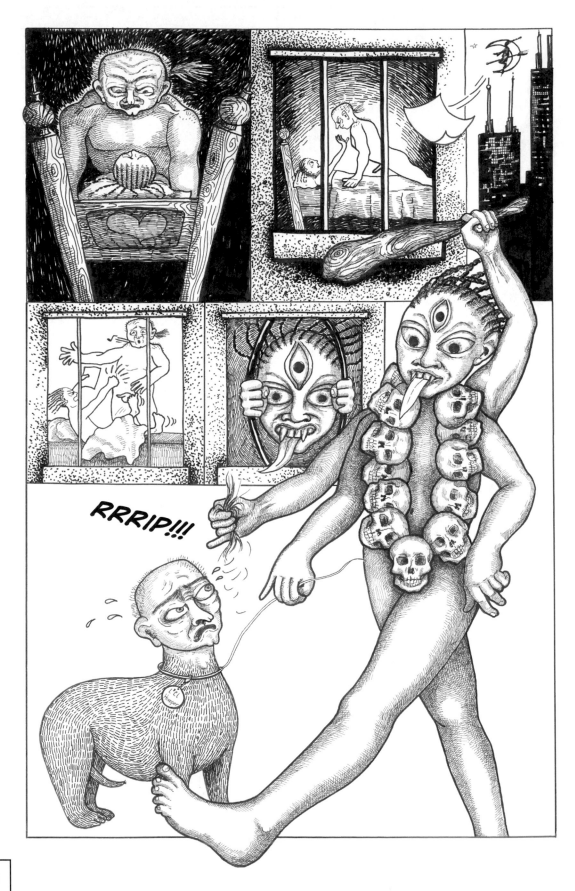

RRRIP!!!

Though revenge was sweet, Mona soon realized that children needed a permanent way to deflate pedophiles.

Obwohl Rache sich hervorragend anfühlte, wusste Mona bald, dass Kinder eine mehr permanente Lösung zu der Kinderbelästigungskrise brauchten.

The children put their minds together.

Die Kinder steckten ihre
Köpfchen zusammen.

Collectively, they decided that all child molesters would be turned into organic, harmless life forms... mushrooms!

Zusammen entschieden sie sich, dass alle Kinderbelästiger zu harmlosen, organischen Lebensformen verwandelt werden sollten... zu Pilzen!

Mona squatted on the damp earth. She felt wonderful.
The mushrooms were perfectly silly! Mona smiled softly.

Mona hockte sich auf den feuchten Erdboden.
Sie fühlte sich wohl. Die Pilze waren total albern!
Mona lächelte leise.

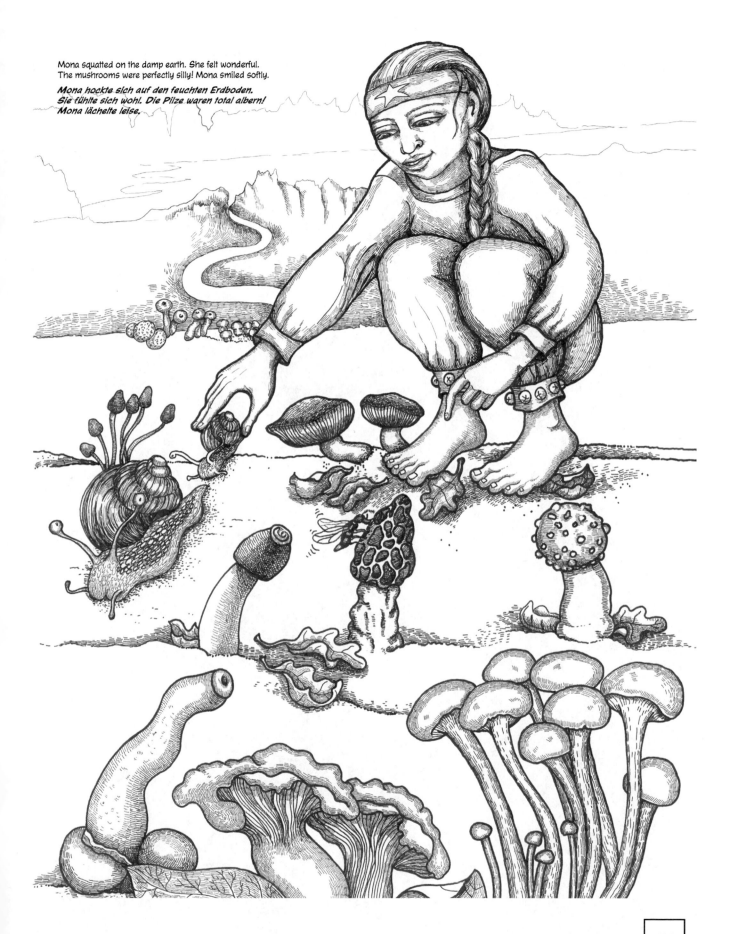

55

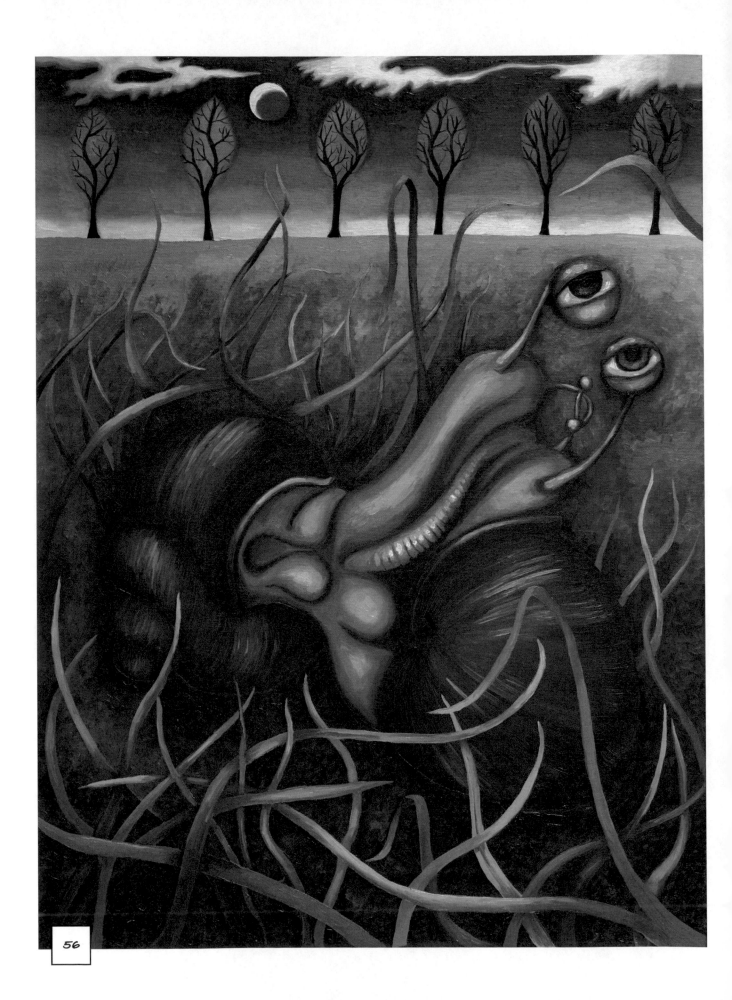

Maisa
& the Most Daring Muslim Women
ميساء والنساء المسلمات الأكثر جرأة

Arabic Translation by Halima Mohammed Abdel Rahman
ترجمة احليمة محمد عبد الرحمن

61

مقدمة

كانت البداية عندما تكرمت صديقة مشتركة بيني والمؤلفة مورين بيردوك بتقديمي إليها في يناير 9002، وكان يحدوني فضول كبير لمعرفة خبايا مشروع البلاغ النسوي وما يتعلق به، وقد أخبرتني صديقتي بأن مورين كانت حينها تكتب رواية، وكانت تبحث عن أفكار لتطوير شخصية بطلة الرواية، والتي هي امرأة مسلمة، مثلي. "بطلة؟" هذا نجاح باهر! تمتمت ببهجة خفية لنفسي. وقد كانت رحلتي مع مورين وما أعقبها من صداقة حميمة ممتعة للغاية، أغنت حياتي بشكل مدهش.

هذه الرواية "ميساء والفتيات المسلمات الأكثر جرأة" تتناول فعلا وحشيا هو "جرائم الشرف" التي ترتكب باسم الدين. بل انه الرعب الذي تواجهه بعض النساء المسلمات ويقاسين منه في ثقافاتهن. مع ذلك وكما سيعلم القراء، الاسلام لم يعلم المسلمين كيف يكونوا قساة القلوب وعنيفين. بل علمنا الله ان نهدي إلى الحق مسترشدين بقلوبنا منابع الحب والتسامح.

أنا إمرأة مسلمة، نشأت والحمد لله في بيئة علمتنا الدين ولم تفرضه علينا فرضاً. فأبي، رغم تشدده الظاهر في تفسير بعض الآيات القرآنية والنصوص الشرعية الأخرى، كان يشجعنا على تكوين فهمنا الخاص لمعاني الدين. بصورة عامة كان فحوى الرسالة التي وصلتنا ان نكون رحماء، عطوفين ومحبين وأن نبعد عن الحكم على الآخرين.

هذه المبادئ ساهمت في توجيهي ليس كإمرأة مسلمة نشأت في امريكا، وانما كإنسان مر بكل الأهوال التى مررت بها في حياتي. إن كان الألم الذي خبرته يبدو غير محتمل ولا يمكن غفرانه، وإن كانت رغبني في الإنتقام لا تقاوم، لكن الدرس الذي تعلمته، والخلاصة التي وصلت إليها تماهت مع الرسالة المضمنة في هذه الرواية: هناك سلام في التسامح. إن الراحة والسلام في الغفران وليس عبر الإنتقام.

في اعتقادي أن هناك خاصية أخرى تمتاز بها هذه الرواية وهي المشاركة، والتي تعد جزءاً أصيلاً لا ينفصل عنها. فالمشاركة تمهد السبيل إلى السلوان و الشفاء. في اعتقادي أن عملية طهي الطعام وتقاسمه مع الآخرين، على بساطتها، تساهم كثيرا في الشفاء. وأنا أحس بسعادة غامرة لأن عملية طهي الطعام تأتي في قلب هذه الرواية، والتي تصور بقوة كيف أن مشاطرة الطعام والحكايات القصصية من الأنشطة الخلاقة، التي تترك آثاراً مدهشة ورائعة في نفوسنا. وبما أن هذه المراسم شكلت جزءا كبيرا من الوسط الثقافي الذي نشأت فيه، فقد ظلت عالقة بذاكرتي إلى اليوم.

إن اتخاذ الصفح والمشاركة والابتكار حلولاً في التغلب على هذه أوغيرها من المصائب، ليست شأناً روائياً بحتاً. فأنا أعيش واتنفس دليلا على أن هذه اطروحات حقيقية لإيجاد السلام والعدالة. آمل من النساء والرجال في جميع انحاء العالم أن يطلعوا ويتشاركوا ويحذقوا في تشكيل الطرق المساعدة في نشر هذه الرسالة القوية. أمل أن تجد النساء اللاتي يؤثر عليهن هذا الأمر أكثر من غيرهن العدالة والسلام الذي ينشدنه.

روبينا كوهين

Dear Arabic reader, please take notice that the panels in this story are meant to be read from left to right.

تنبيه

عزيزي القارئ/عزيزتي القارئة

أنوه إلى "أنه يمكن قراءة الأطر الحاوية للنصوص في هذه الرواية من اليسار الى اليمين!

Introduction
Rubina Cohen

When a mutual friend introduced me to Maureen Burdock in January 2009, I was curious to find out what *The F Word Project* was all about. My friend told me Maureen was writing a novel, and she was looking for ideas as she developed the heroine of the story, who was Muslim, as I am. "A heroine? Wow!" I thought to myself. The journey I have taken with Maureen and the friendship that has ensued have enriched my life tremendously.

This fable, "Maisa & the Most Daring Muslim Women," is about the heartless act of "honor killings" in the name of Allah. Yes, this is a horror that some Muslim women have to live with and endure in their culture. Yet, as readers will learn, Islam does not teach Muslims to be heartless and violent. In fact, we are taught to lead with our hearts, from a place of love and forgiveness.

I am a Muslim woman who was raised, thankfully, in a household where religion was taught but not imposed on us. My father, though strict in reading and interpreting passages from the Qur'an and other Islamic texts, also encouraged us to find our own meaning. Generally, the message we were given was to be kind, gentle, and loving, and not to judge others.

These principles have guided me not just as a Muslim woman growing up in America but also as a human being who has been through my own horrors in life. At the time, what I was going through seemed unbearable and unforgivable, and I wanted revenge. Yet the lessons I have learned, and the conclusions I have come to, are in line with the message that comes through in this fable: there is justice in forgiving. It's not through revenge but through forgiving that one will find peace and heal.

Another big piece for me was about sharing, which is an integral part of this story. Sharing offers yet another path to solace and healing. For me, the simple act of cooking and sharing food with others has brought so much healing, and I am thrilled that cooking is at the heart of this story. It powerfully illustrates how the creative acts of sharing food and stories can have wondrous and miraculous effects on our souls. Having been a big part of the culture I was raised in, sharing such sustenance remains important to me today.

Forgiving, sharing, and creating, as solutions to cope with this and other kinds of calamity, are not just for fiction writing. I am living and breathing proof that these are true paths to finding peace and justice. I hope that women and men around the world read, share, and create ways to spread the word about this powerful message. I hope that the women this touches the most find the justice and peace they are searching for.

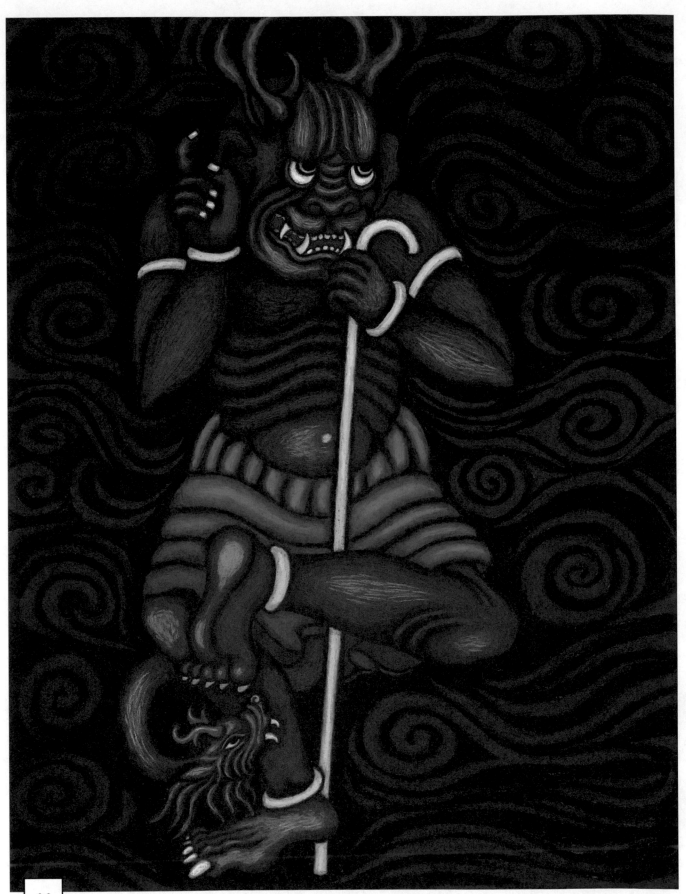

Maisa is buried in her coffin, but she cannot rest.

ميساء ممددة في نعشها ولكنها تبدو غير مرتاحة.

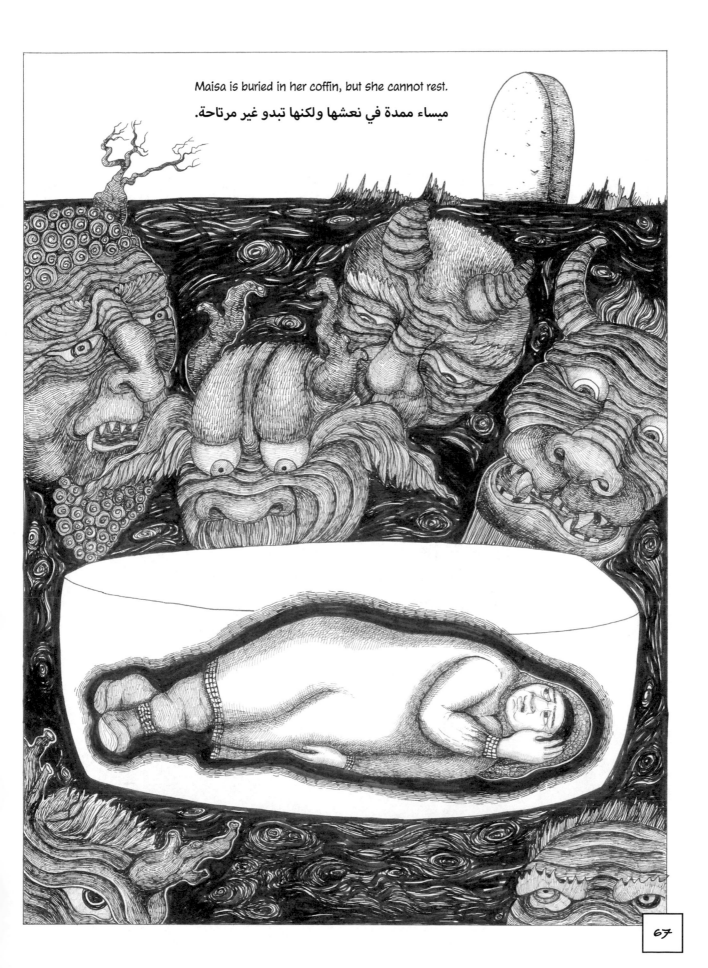

67

Suddenly. . .

فجأة..

Maisa is very disoriented and can't remember how she died. Her djinn, Little Maisa, tells her what happened:

تبدو ميساء شديدة التشويش، و لا تذكر كيف رحلت عن الدنيا. فتقوم جنيتها ،ميساء الصغيرة باخبارها:

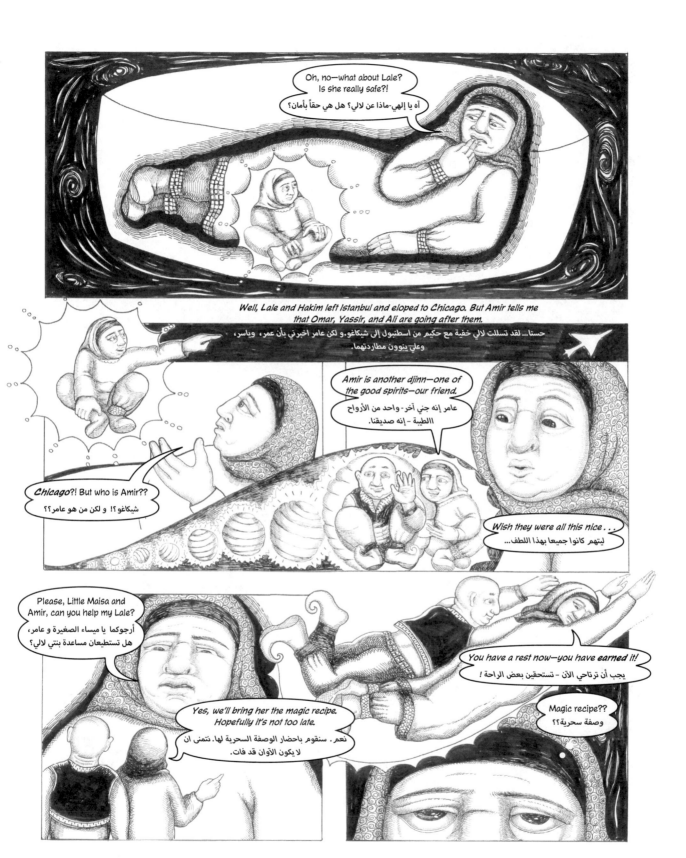

73

Quickly, he snatches back the mint...

و بسرعة، يقوم بخطف النعناع...

...and drops it into the magic soup...

ويضيفه إلى الحساء السحري...

...just as Uncle Omar and his dreadful sons, Ali and Yassir, arrive.

في اللحظة التي يصل فيها الخال عمر وولديه البغيضين، علي و ياسر.

Quickly, Lale, eat!
Um, there's just one thing you should know ...

بسرعة يا لالي كُلي! ممم، هنالك شى يجب عليك معرفته.

I feel really strange

ينتابني إحساس غريب

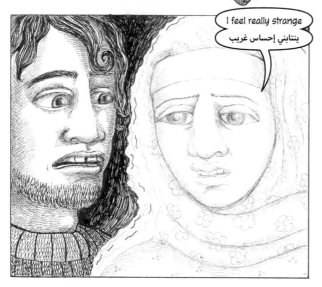

BAM
BAM
BAM

طرق على الباب طاخ طاخ طاخ

AWWW... Let me get that for you!
Coming all this way from Turkey, and they don't let you in! For shame.

آوووو... أسمحوا لي بإحضار هذا لكم. لقد قطعتم كل هذه المسافة من تركيا، و لم يسمحوا لكم حتى بالدخول! يا للعار.

75

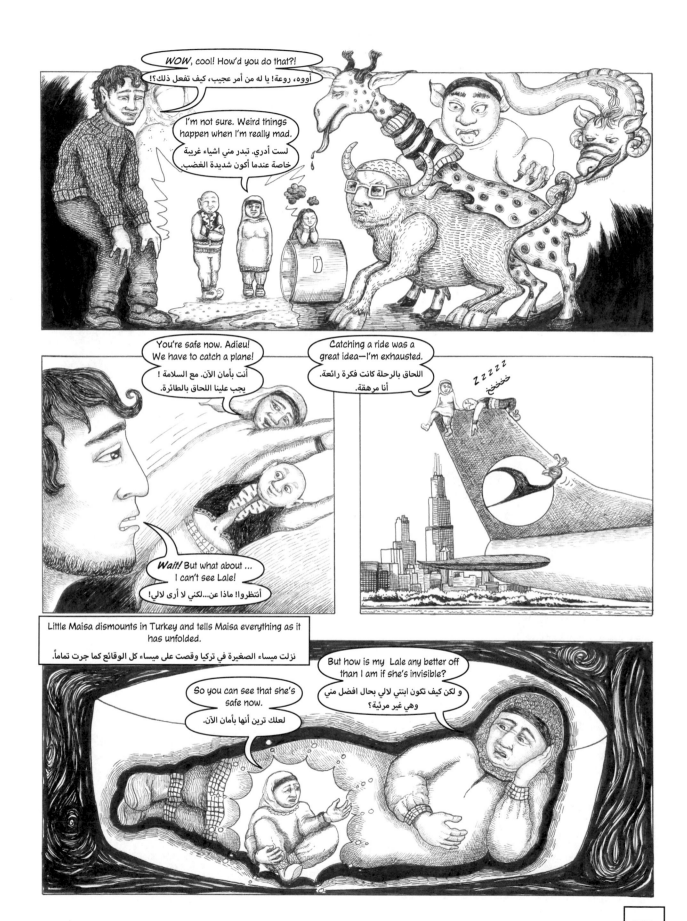

Well, I don't know the magic recipe for visibility. But I met this djinn in Egypt once who knows it. Amir went to find her.

حسناً، لا علم لي بالوصفة السحرية للإظهار. و لكنني ذات مرة، قابلت جنية في مصر لها معرفة بها. لقد ذهب عامر للبحث عنها.

Whooo?? A simurgh*?!

من؟؟ سيمورغ؟

* A Persian mythical winged creature, female, benevolent, and gigantic enough to carry off an elephant or a whale.

*السيمورغ هي مخلوقة أسطورية فارسية ذات أجنحة، محسنة، وعملاقة بما يكفي لحمل فيل او حوت على ظهرها.

You're taking me to Cairo?

هل ستأخذينني إلى القاهرة؟

Kraah kraaah!

كاك كاااك!

Hello, sphinx. How did a beautiful creature like you lose your nose*?

* مرحبا بأم الهول. كيف خسرت مخلوقة جميلة مثلك أنفها؟

*There have been many theories about how the great Sphinx of Giza lost her nose. It is believed that the nose was destroyed in 1378 by a Sufi fanatic, Muhammad Sa'im al-Dahr, who, enraged by the lifelike representation of a human face, ordered the nose be removed.

هناك العديد من التفسيرات للكيفية التي فقدت بها أم الهول أنفها. هناك اعتقاد سائد بأن صوفي متطرف اسمه محمد صائم الدهر قام سنة 8731 بتهشيم أنف أم الهول وذلك في احدى فورات غضبه لمحاكاة وجهها بالوجه البشري.

78

Later that day, the simurgh and Amir land in a crowded Cairo market.

لاحقا في ذلك اليوم، حط السيمورغ و عامر في أحد أسواق القاهرة المزدحمة.

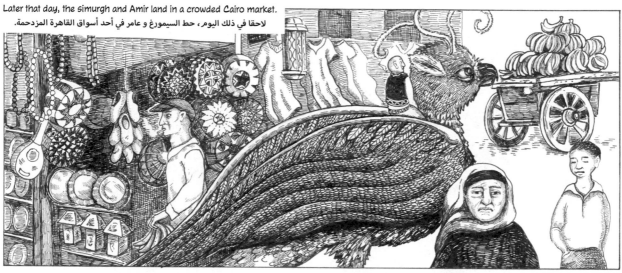

Greetings! I'm looking for the magic recipe that will make women visible.

سلامات،أنا أبحث عن الوصفة السحرية التي تظهر النساء المخفيات.

Why would women want to be visible?! It only brings trouble. Look what our husbands did to us because we were too visible!

لماذا تريد النساءالمخفيات أن يكن مرئيات؟ إن ذلك لا يجلب سوى المتاعب. أنظرن ماذا فعل بنا أزواجنا لأننا كنا مرئيات جداً!

HEE HEE HAHAHA!!

هِهِي هَههههه!!

Mine thought men were looking at me, so he cut off my nose!

لقد شك زوجي في أن الرجال ينظرون إلَّ، فما كان منه إلا أن قام بجدع انفي!

Mine thought I was looking at other men, so he gouged out my eyes. To preserve his honor, he said.

أما أنا فقد ظن زوجي أني استرق النظر إلى الرجال الآخرين، فما كان منه إلا أن قام باقتلاع عينيَّ، وقال إنه فعل ذلك حفاظاً على شرفه.

CAWW!

I understand the problem!
أنا اتفهم الوضع!

Amina and Sara's father accused them of being bad Muslim girls. Making them invisible with my magic lamb meatball recipe was the only way I could save them from his bullets!

اتهم والد أمينة وسارة بنتيه بأنهما فتاتين مسلمتين طائشتين. فما كان مني إلا أن جعلتهما خفيتين باستخدام وصفة مصباح كرات اللحم السحري، خاصتي، كانت تلك هي الطريقة الوحيدة لإنقاذ حياتهما من أعيرته النارية.

I, too, am looking for this recipe. I don't know it, but I did meet a djinn in Pakistan once who does...

أنا أيضا أبحث عن هذه الوصفة. لكني لا أعرفها، غير أني قابلت جنياً في إحدى المرات في باكستان يعرف بأمرها.

Come with us to Pakistan. Maybe the djinn there can help you, too.

تعالي معنا إلى باكستان. ربما تستطيع الجنية هناك مساعدتك أيضاً.

KARAH! KARAH!
كرا! كرا!

The simurgh and her cargo make a detour to Turkey before heading to Pakistan.

تتوقف السيمورغ بحمولتها في تركيا قبل إستئناف رحلتها إلى باكستان.

The simurgh descends at a temple ruin in Pakistan. A group of invisible women is gathered here, and...

يحط السيمورغ في حطام أحد المعابد في باكستان. و كان هناك تجمع لنساء غير منظورات، و.....

RABIA?!?

ربيعة؟!؟

Yasmine, is this the djinn you brought us all this way to see?

ياسمين، هل قطعنا كل هذه المسافة لنرى هذه الجنية؟

Why, yes... You know each other?

في الواقع، نعم... هل تعرفان بعضكما بعضاً؟

Hello, Rabia, we've come to ask you for the magic recipe that will make women visible again.

مرحبا ربيعة، لقد أتينا لنسألكم عن الوصفةالسحرية التي تساعد النساء المخفيات على أن يصبحن مرئيات مجددا.

Magic recipe? There is no magic recipe.

وصفة سحرية؟ لا توجد لدينا وصفة سحرية.

We came all the way here—for THIS?!?

هل قطعنا كل هذه المسافة - لأجل هذا؟!؟

The only way to make the women visible again is to bring them all together.

الطريقة الوحيدة لجعل النساء مرئيات مجددا هي بجلبهن جميعاً.

The bad Muslim girls must cook the recipes that made them invisible. Sharing all of their magic foods with each other will make them visible once more—to each other and to the world.

على الفتيات المسلمات الطائشات طبخ الوصفات التي جعلتهن غير منظورات، ثم تقاسمها مع بعضهن البعض ليصبحن مرئيات إلى بعضهن أولاً ثم إلى الناس.

And why would we ever trust *YOU* again, after the dirty tricks you've played?!?

و لماذا ينبغي علينا أن نثق بك مجددا، بعد كل تلك الحيل الدنيئة التي مارستها علينا؟!؟

Well, haha, you don't really have a choice, do you?

حسناً، ليس لديكن خيار آخر، هههه، أليس كذلك؟

And for that matter, neither do these bad Muslim girls who have come to me: Shirin, Ratima, Nasrin, Aisha, Shamim, Zulekha, and Fatima.

لا بالنسبة لهذه المسألة، ولا بالنسبة لأولئك الفتيات المسلمات الطائشات أمثال شيرين، ورتيمة، ونسرين، وعائشة، وشميم، وزليخا، وفاطمة، اللائي أتين إليَّ.

GRRR... Okay then, everyone on board—we're going to Chicago.

قررر...حسناً إذن، ليصعد الجميع- سنذهب إلى شيكاغو.

85

Moments later...

بعد لحظات...

Oh, my poor little Lale! Even invisible, I still know my daughter!

أوه، ابنتي لالي الصغيرة المسكينة! استطيع التعرف عليها حتى ولو كانت خفية!

Maisa!! You're *alive*?!?

ميساء هل أنتِ حيّة ترزقين؟!؟

Yes, when the simurgh pulled me out of the grave, I woke up!

نعم، لقد إستيقظت عندما سحبني السيمورغ خارج القبر.

All right, enough reminiscing— you have a lot of cooking to do!

حسناً، يكفي استرجاعاً للذكريات، لديكن طبيخ كثير لتنجزنه!

عدس

87

After many hours of cooking, the group gathers in Lale and Hakim's living room for a big feast. Surprisingly, the rascal Rabia Djinn had told them the truth. As the women share their magic foods, each one of them regains her visibility. They laugh and share their stories for hours.

بعد عدة ساعات من القيام بأعمال المطبخ، إتأمر شمل الجميع في غرفة المعيشة استعداداً للوليمة الكبرى. فجأة اعترفت ربيعة الجنية الشريرة بالحقيقة. وفي اثناء تقاسم النساء أطباق الطعام السحري استعادت كل واحدة منهن مرئيتها، وامضين عدة ساعات في الضحك وتبادل الحكايات.

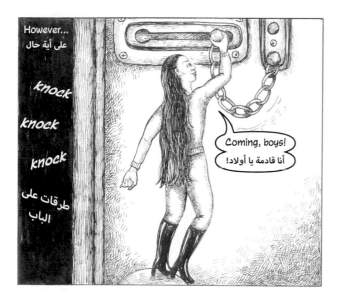

89

We don't deserve your forgiveness.

نحن غير جديرين بعفوك

What we have done is unforgiveable.

ماارتكبناه من جرم لا يغتفر

We are the only bad Muslims here.

نحن المسلمون الوحيدون السيئون هنا.

Please, please forgive us!

ارجوكي ارجوكي سامحينا!

(سورة الشورى 24)

QUR'AN
SURAH 42

42:40 The recompense for an injury is an injury equal thereto {in degree}: but if a person forgives and makes reconciliation, his or her reward is due from Allah: for {Al-lah} loveth not those who do wrong.

42:41 But indeed if any do help and defend themselves after a wrong {done} to them, against such there is no cause of blame.

42:42 The blame is only against those who oppress others with wrong-doing and insolently transgress beyond bounds through the land, defying right and justice: for such there will be a penalty grievous.

42:43 But indeed if any show patience and forgive, that would truly be an exercise of courageous will and resolution in the conduct of affairs.

(وَجَزَاءُ سَيِّئَةٍ سَيِّئَةٌ مِّثْلُهَا فَمَنْ عَفَا وَأَصْلَحَ فَأَجْرُهُ عَلَى اللَّهِ إِنَّهُ لَا يُحِبُّ الظَّالِمِينَ (40) وَلَمَنِ انتَصَرَ بَعْدَ ظُلْمِهِ فَأُولَٰئِكَ مَا عَلَيْهِم مِّن سَبِيلٍ (41) إِنَّمَا السَّبِيلُ عَلَى الَّذِينَ يَظْلِمُونَ النَّاسَ وَيَبْغُونَ فِي الْأَرْضِ بِغَيْرِ الْحَقِّ أُولَٰئِكَ لَهُم عَذَابٌ أَلِيمٌ (42) وَلَمَن صَبَرَ وَغَفَرَ إِنَّ ذَٰلِكَ لَمِنْ عَزْمِ الْأُمُورِ (43)

In the spirit of the QUR'AN, and because she is compassionate and kind, Maisa serves the remorseful men tea from the samovar that Omar had once hurled at Lale and her in blind fury.

بروح القرآن المتسامحة، ولأنها رحيمة وعطوفة، فقد قامت ميساء بصب الشاي إلى الرجال الذين تآكلهم الندم، من نفس الابريق الذي كان عمر قد قذفها هي ولالي به في احدى فورات غضبه.

And they celebrate late into the night—good Muslim girls, women, men, and djinns, all together.

ثم إحتفل الجميع - الفتيات المسلمات الطيبات، والنساء والرجال والجنيون إلى وقت متأخر من الليل.

Mumbi & the Long Run

Mumbi Na Mbiyo Za Masafa Marefu

Swahili Translation by David Opiyo

Introduction
Helen Concannon

While researching for creative ways of presenting the sensitive topic of female circumcision, I came across Maureen Burdock and her innovative *F Word Project*. When I contacted her she was mid-writing "Mumbi & the Long Run" and I was immediately captured by her passion and innovation in addressing the taboo subject of female circumcision.

Having worked with the women of Londiani, Kenya, I had been privileged to hear their stories, listen to their histories and learn about this deep-rooted cultural practice from their communities. Working in partnership with the communities, Friends of Londiani developed an Alternative Rite of Passage like the one described by Mumbi. It's accepted locally by the communities because they helped design it, taking into account the research from other organizations. The ARP incorporates all the traditional teachings and cultural sharing that the traditional circumcision does, except it does it without any cutting and therefore no health risks. When I read Mumbi and saw how Maureen had intertwined so many important topics together, I loved how this simulated the reality facing young girls and women around the world. Everything is interconnected—circumcision, early marriage, education, health. Maureen has brought these important life choices to us through the wonderful medium of the comic book, making it an educational tool for girls to read and learn through.

I commend Maureen for her inspiration to use graphic art to address some of the important issues facing girls and women in today's world. It's not only Mumbi who has courage, Maureen has also shown courage in highlighting an Alternative Rite of Passage which is a successful way of changing one of our cultural practices.

96

Moments after waking from her dream, Mumbi hops out of bed, not wanting to dwell on sad memories. She steps into the kitchen, where she finds her housemates already enjoying chai and bread.

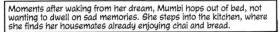

Masaa fupi baada ya kuamuka, kutoka ndoto yake, mumbi yuaruka toka kitanda yake kwa vile hataki kufikiria makaye yaliopita kutoka chimba cha kulala, mumbi alielekea jikoni ambapo alikutana wenzake wanaoburudika na kiamshakinywa ya chai kwa mkate.

Good morning Sam, Gracie! An easy 10 miles today?

Habari ya asubuhi sa, Gracie! Leo tukimbie maili kumi?

Morning. Yeah, Rail Trail.

Habari Mumbi, hiyo ni sawa njia la gari la moshi ni sawa.

We were so close. We used to talk about *everything*. She was so beautiful, too, all soft and round and lovely.

Tulipendana sana, kati yetu tuliongea bila kuficha lolote. Alikuwa mrembo piya, ngozi Nyororo na umbo linayofurahisha sana.

You miss her a *lot*, don't you... Unamfikiria sana. Sivyo...

Yeah, of course. Even though she used to tease me that my hair sticks out like electrical wires!

Kweli jameni uingawa alikuwa ananitumia ati Nywele yangu yamesimama kama miti ya waya za stima!

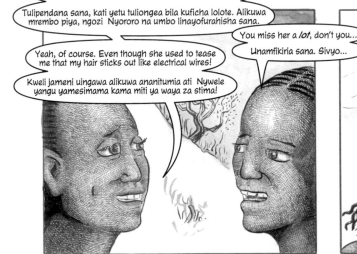

A short while later, the three runners are on Santa Fe's Rail Trail, warming up in the brisk hour before dawn.

Masaa fupi baadaye, Hawa wanariadha watatu waelekea njia la reli ya Santa Fe, ote kwa hewa safi la asubui.

You're more serious than usual, Mumbi.

Leo waonokana unafikiria makubwa Mumbi.

Yeah, I dreamed about my sister, Makena.

Ni kweli kabisa, jana nilioata ndoto la dadangu, Makena.

Well it *does*! Na ni kweli tena!

Does what?! Ukweli gani?!

Stick out like wires! Waya ya stima!

Not *you*, too! Siyo Nawe pia!

Like brother and sister, you two! Nyinyi wawili ni ndugu na dada!

Later that day, Mumbi meets Dustin, her manager, at the high school track.

Baadaye siku hiyo, Mumbi alikutana na Dustin, Meneja wake, kwenye uwanja wa shule.

Time to get you up to SPEED for that Berlin Marathon. Only eight weeks to go!

Saa imefika ya kujulisha yanayojiri kuhusu mbiyo za Berlin Marathon, wiki nane pekee!

800 meter laps—my favorite. Hahaha!

Mbiyo za mita mia nane, nayapenda sana! Hahaha!

WOW!!! LAHAULA!!!!

Dang! Where'd SHE come from?!

Dang! Na HUYU dada ametokezea wapi?!

Four 800s to go at 2:06 pace!

Lapu nne za mia nane ya me baki ukikimbia kwa dakika 2:06!

Great job today. You're "on track." Hahaha!

Umefanya kazi nzuri leo .Umeshika njia sambamba" Hahaha!

Time for a massage...

Nisaa ya kupoesha misuli...

Water? Maji?

No. Thanks. La, ahsante.

The following morning, Mumbi, Sam, and Gracie catch a train down to Albuquerque.

Ke2sho yake, Mumbi, Sam na Gracie wapanda wote gari la moshi wakielekea Albuquerque.

Ready for 18 miles today?

Uko tayari kukimbia maili 18 leo?

A while later, the friends arrive at the Bosque and begin warming up.

Dakika chache badaye, marafiki zao wafika kwenye. Busaye ambapo wote wanza kukimbia kunyoosha misuli.

Mumbi, you are so quiet today.

Mumbi, leo uko kimya kweli.

It's so sad what happened to your sister. Now female genital cutting is illegal in Kenya.

Yasikitisha sana yale yalio pata dadako. Kwa sasa, ukeke taji ya wanawake ni kinyume cha sheria nchini Kenya.

Yeah, I'm still thinking about the dream of Makena I had the other day.

Ndiyo, bado nafikiria lile ndoto juu ya Makena niliyokuwa nayo juzi.

Yes, but change comes slowly, even with laws in place.

Sawa, lakini mabadiliko huja pole pole, hata kama kunayo sheria kabambe

I told my aunt about a different rite of passage that a group there called Harambe is putting together. But they still need money to make the alternative rites happen. Unless they get help fast, Esther will have to go through the traditional rite.

Nilimwambia mamangu mdogo juu ya njia tofauti kutoka utoto kuwa mwanamke ambayo kikundi kinacho itwa Harambe wanaanzisha. Lakini bado wanaitaji pesa kuwezesha hayo mila badala. Wasipo pata usadizi kwa haraka, itabidi Esther apitie mila za kitamaduni ya ukeke taji.

Eighteen miles later...

Maili 18 baadae

What are you going to do?

Utafanya nini?

I have to win some races, make money!

Lazima ni yashinde mbio kadhaa, ni pate pesa!

103

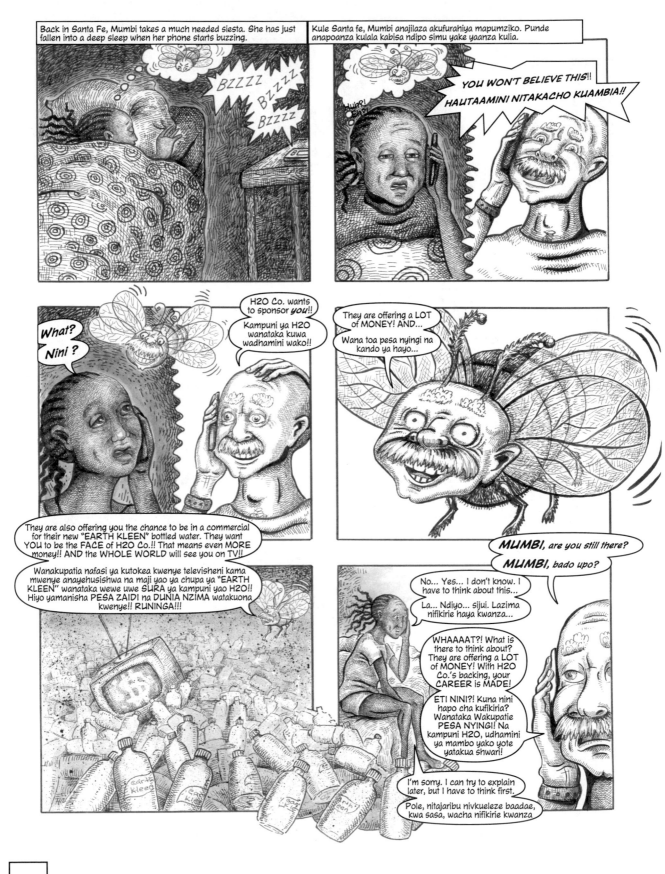

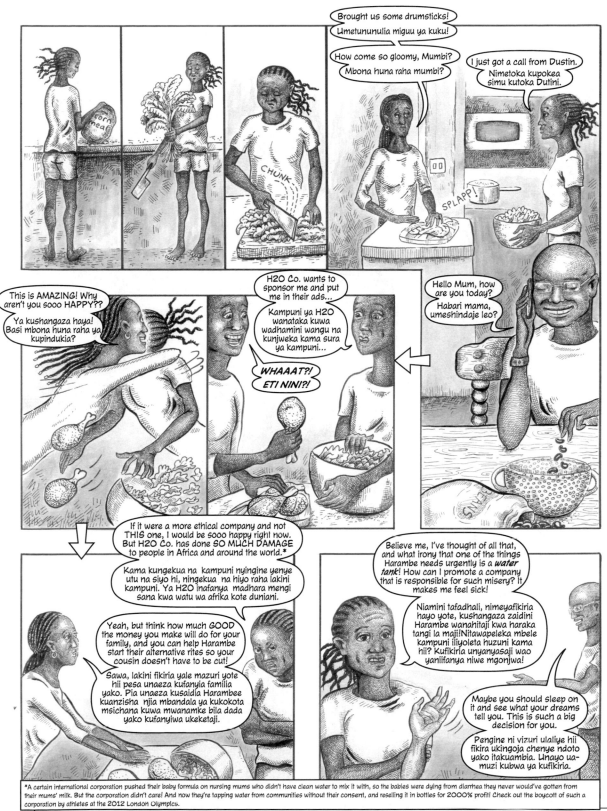

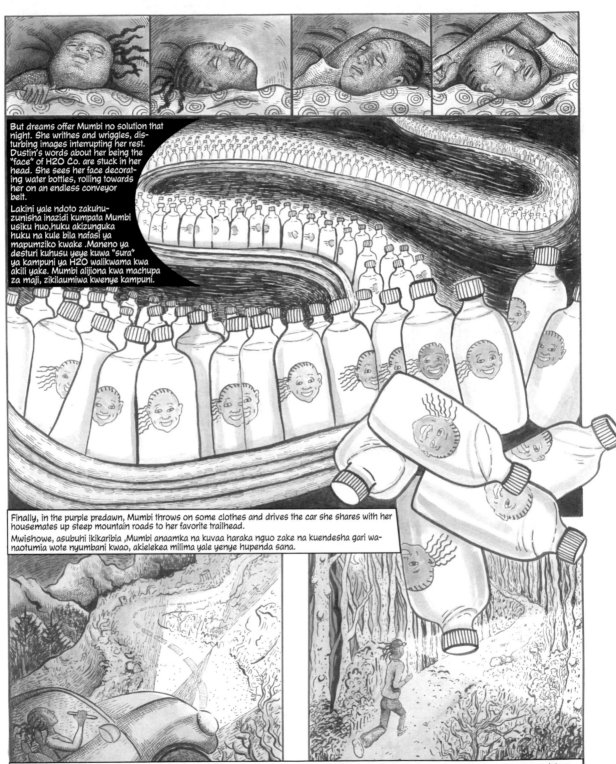

But dreams offer Mumbi no solution that night. She writhes and wriggles, disturbing images interrupting her rest. Dustin's words about her being the "face" of H2O Co. are stuck in her head. She sees her face decorating water bottles, rolling towards her on an endless conveyor belt.

Lakini yale ndoto zakuhuzunisha inazidi kumpata Mumbi usiku huo, huku akizunguka huku na kule bila nafasi ya mapumziko kwake. Maneno ya desturi kuhusu yeye kuwa "sura" ya kampuni ya H2O walikwama kwa akili yake. Mumbi alijiona kwa machupa za maji, zikilaumiwa kwenye kampuni.

Finally, in the purple predawn, Mumbi throws on some clothes and drives the car she shares with her housemates up steep mountain roads to her favorite trailhead.

Mwishowe, asubuhi ikikaribia ,Mumbi anaamka na kuvaa haraka nguo zake na kuendesha gari wanaotumia wote nyumbani kwao, akielekea milima yale yenye hupenda sana.

As Mumbi begins to climb, the bright beam of her headlamp illuminates roots and rocks along the trail. She hopes it will frighten away any predators, as well. Running alone in the wilderness, especially at night, is not something she would normally do, but this is the best way she can think of to clear her mind.

Vile Mumbi anaanza kupanda milima, mataa za gari yakimulika mawe za mlima na matawi hapo anadhania atawafukuza walio na nia mbaya. Kukimbia pekeyake huko mlimani siyo kitu anaweza kufanya pekeyake, lakini hapa ndiyo mafikira zake hutulia kilamara akikimbiya hapa.

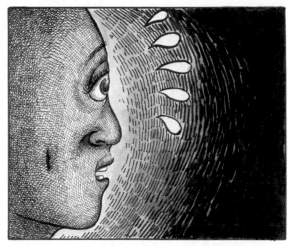

107

Mumbi has never in her life run as fast as she is running down the trail now, after seeing the mountain lion. But despite—or maybe because of—the shock she's just had, everything is suddenly very clear to her.

Mumbi hajawai kukimbia kwa kasi vile anavyokimbia leo, baada ya kuona jumba anayopatikana mlimani. Lakini licha ya, ama kwasababu ya, ile mshtuko aliyopata kwa kuona simba, yale yote hayangeona, sasa yamemulikwa.

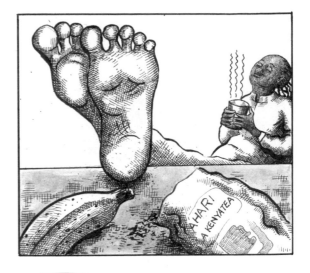

Hi, Dustin.

Habari Destin.

Well, Mumbi, have you come to your senses I hope?

Mumbi, niambie umefikia suluhisho ile itakayo kufaa?

Yes, I have decided. I'm sorry, but I won't be the face of H2O Co.

Ndio, nimeamua. Pole lakini sitakua "sura" la kampuni ya H2O.

I will just have to make sure I place in Berlin.

Ya bidi nipate nafasi kwa mkondo wa Berlin.

Please don't call me "Kiddo." I am almost 30 years old.

Tafadhali usiniite mwanako, mimi nakaribia miaka 30.

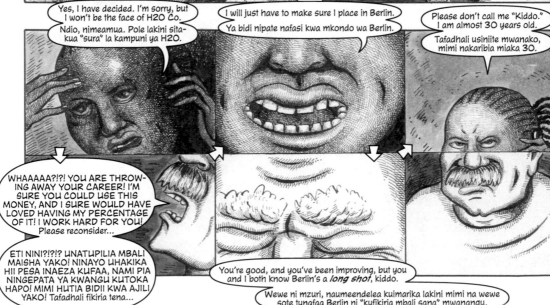

WHAAAAA?!?! YOU ARE THROWING AWAY YOUR CAREER! I'M SURE YOU COULD USE THIS MONEY, AND I SURE WOULD HAVE LOVED HAVING MY PERCENTAGE OF IT! I WORK HARD FOR YOU! Please reconsider...

ETI NINI?!?!? UNATUPILIA MBALI MAISHA YAKO! NINAYO UHAKIKA HII PESA INAEZA KUFAA, NAMI PIA NINGEPATA YA KWANGU KUTOKA HAPO! MIMI HUTIA BIDII KWA AJILI YAKO! Tafadhali fikiria tena...

You're good, and you've been improving, but you and I both know Berlin's a *long shot*, kiddo.

Wewe ni mzuri, naumeendelea kuimarika lakini mimi na wewe sote tunafaa Berlin ni "kufikiria mbali sana" mwanangu.

108

A short while later, Mumbi video calls her family in Kenya.
Muda mfupi baadae, Mumbi awasiliana kwa njia ya picha na familia yake nchini Kenya.

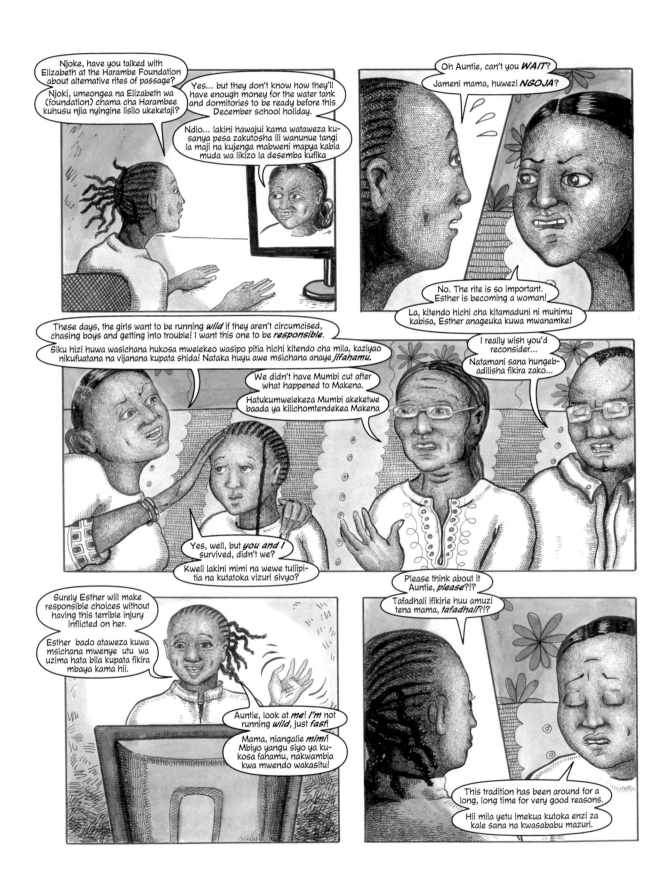

After the talk with her family, Mumbi knows what she must do. She has made a tough decision, and now her direction is as clear as the new day she wakes up to the following morning. She must train hard—harder than ever before in her life.

Baada yakuongea na familia yake, Mumbi sasa anafahamu ile tazuma afanye. Amefikia uamuzi kubwa na sasa njia yake umejitokeza kwa uhakika kama siku mpya anayoamukia kesho. Lazima afanye zoezi zaidi,akiweka bidii kushinda siku zingine zote amewahi kufanya mazoezi.

Mumbi puts everything she has into it. She charges up and down steep mountains to build leg strength and endurance, and tears up the local running track to increase her speed. She averages more than 80 miles per week over the next few weeks.

Mumbi anaweka yote anayo kwenye anachotaka kutimiza, akipanda na kushuka mulima kufunga nguvu yake na uvumilivu wa mwili wake.kuongeza mwendo wake waukasi.anafikia maili 80 kwa wiki muda huu.

*In 2011, the International Association of Athletics Federations made a controversial decision that men would no longer be allowed to pace women at races.

*Katika mwaka wa 2011, jumuia ya kimataifa ya wanariadha (IAAF) walimeia uamuzi uliyo zaautata kua wanaume hawataruhusiwa tena kuwa wakupangia wanawake mwendo kwenye mbiyo.

*Döner Kebabs are delicious Turkish sandwiches sold by many vendors around Berlin.

*Kababu za Doner ni nyama umeandaliwa katikati ya mikate kutoka nchi ya uturuki,na wenye viosk wengi wanaviuaza huku Berlin.

118

The morning of the Berlin Marathon has arrived. Tens of thousands of runners gather at the start.
Asubuhi ya siku ya Berlin marathon imefika.ma elfu ya wanariadha wanajikusanya wakiwa tayari kuanza.

The streets of Berlin are packed with spectators. For Mumbi, their voices are a distant buzz.

Barabara vya Berlin vimejaa na mashabiki. Kwake mumbi, sauti yao yanamfikia kwa umbali.

She focuses on staying with the leaders as the pack of elite women racers thins out.

Nia yake ni kuhaakikisha anakimbiya na wale wanariadha wenye ujuzi vile tayari wanaanza kijitenganisha.

Mumbi hears the breaths and footfalls of another runner close behind her. She is distracted for a moment. In her mind, she begins to chant Esther's name to the rhythm of her own even footsteps.

Mumbi anaskia vile mwanariadha mwenzake anavyo pumua na vile miguu yanavyo shika lami.

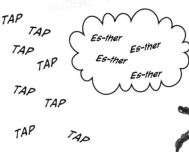

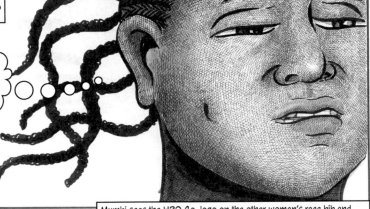

But moments later, a runner manages to pass her.

Lakini dakika chache baadae, mwanariadha moja yuampita Mumbi.

Mumbi sees the H2O Co. logo on the other woman's race bib and feels a surge of fury!

Mumbi yuaona alama ya kampuni ya H2O Co. ikiwa imeandikwa kwenye vazi la kukimbia la huyo mwanariadha na haapo ndiyo hasira yake yazidi!

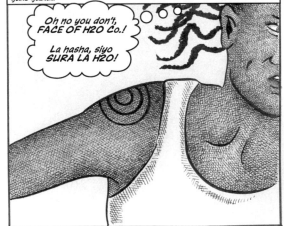

Oh no you don't, FACE OF H2O Co.!

La hasha, siyo SURA LA H2O!

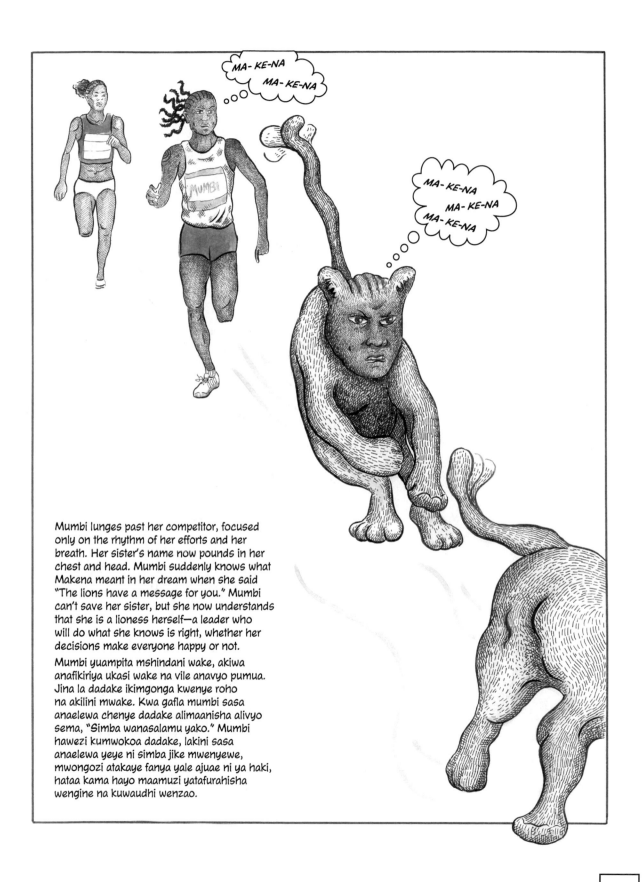

Mumbi lunges past her competitor, focused only on the rhythm of her efforts and her breath. Her sister's name now pounds in her chest and head. Mumbi suddenly knows what Makena meant in her dream when she said "The lions have a message for you." Mumbi can't save her sister, but she now understands that she is a lioness herself—a leader who will do what she knows is right, whether her decisions make everyone happy or not.

Mumbi yuampita mshindani wake, akiwa anafikiriya ukasi wake na vile anavyo pumua. Jina la dadake ikimgonga kwenye roho na akilini mwake. Kwa gafla mumbi sasa anaelewa chenye dadake alimaanisha alivyo sema, "Simba wanasalamu yako." Mumbi hawezi kumwokoa dadake, lakini sasa anaelewa yeye ni simba jike mwenyewe, mwongozi atakaye fanya yale ajuae ni ya haki, hataa kama hayo maamuzi yatafurahisha wengine na kuwaudhi wenzao.

Mumbi sees nothing but her goal as she charges towards the finish line. All uncertainty and sadness have left her in this timeless moment of fearless motion.

Mumbi haoni mengine yote kuliko lengo lake akikaribia laini ya kumaliza.yale yote aliyokua akishuku na kutokuaa na uhaakika yote yapotea anavyo pata nguvu bila uoga.

But it is Mumbi's human form, sweating and nearly past the point of total exhaustion, that crosses the finish line—in first place among the women.

Lakini mumbi ni mwanadamu, huku akitoa jasho na akikaribia ujovu kisicho na kipimo.

Sam, who placed third overall, and Dustin, who is beside himself with amazement, embrace her with tears of joy.

Sam, mwenye sasa ni nambari tatu kwa jumla, na Dustin, mwenye ameshikwa na mshangao, amkumbatia kwa raha na machozi.

O WOW WOW WOW WOW...

I always knew you could do it!

Nilijua utaweza, si-kushuku hata kidogo!!

Esther, *we did it*!

Esther, tumefanikiwa!

Study hard and aim *high*, because *anything* is possible!

Soma kwa bidii na lenga juu, kwa vile yote yawezekana!

Afterword
Esther Korir with Norah Sirma

I am an avid fan of *The F Word Project*: I love the humor that is brought out by the characters about serious topics. I was recently glued to one of the comics written by Maureen Burdock. "Mumbi & the Long Run" has really captured my imagination and I am sure it will capture millions of other people around the world. It is a very good tool for teaching and for use by facilitators in the Alternative Rites of Passage programs.

"Mumbi & the Long Run" is about eliminating the practice of female genital mutilation/cutting (FGM/C) and early marriage in an increasingly globalized world like Kenya. Having been raised here, I know it is a big part of our culture and FGM/C has been practiced traditionally in our African culture in most of our communities. This practice is highly valued as it is believed to give girls and women dignity, respect and mainly enable them to get husbands and thus, a sense of belonging to the community. As a teaching tool "Mumbi & the Long Run" highlights the impacts of FGM/C positively and negatively, with an important emphasis on the benefits of alternative rites of passage (ARP).

I have been facilitating trainings on Alternative Rites of Passage for a while in some of the communities in Kenya and one big thing I have learned is that to change our lives, we must be prepared to confront our fears and worries, and to embrace courage. Thankfully, "Mumbi & the Long Run" emphasizes the alternative rite of passage, which embraces a positive message, since it is against cutting. Change is a huge challenge in most of our cultures. Thus courage is very important for the girls and women in our communities to develop during the Alternative Rites of Passage trainings. Courage gives wings to girls and women to set them free to fly like they have never been able to fly.

Mumbi in the long run broke her own record and became part of a world-record-breaking event that will probably be unmatched for many years to come. By going against the odds and thus embracing Alternative Rites of Passage, this shows that you can put actions and attitude into one word: Courage.

Embracing Alternative Rites of Passage is the only solution to get girls and women to pursue their dreams, to make their own decisions, to know their rights and take charge of their own lives, thus being able to raise good families. "Mumbi & the Long Run" and other such stories can help facilitators of the ARP by desensitizing the formerly taboo topic, so that men and women can more comfortably discuss the issues and arrive at a clear and deep understanding of the need for such change.

In the spirit of Mumbi, girls and women go on—be courgeous, step out of your comfort zone, take that action you are afraid of taking—it could be the key to your success.

Esther Korir and Norah Sirma are facilitators of the Alternative Rite of Passage with Friends of Londiani Kenya.

Halima's Story

A Future without Female Genital Mutilation

Written by Halima Mohamed Abdel Rahman
Art by Maureen Burdock

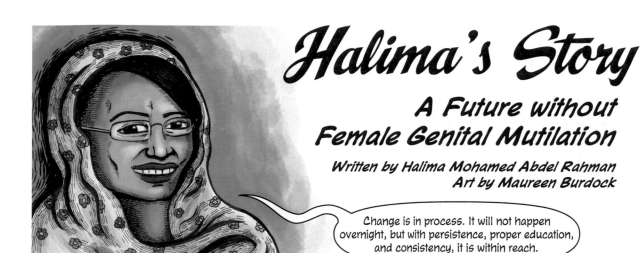

Change is in process. It will not happen overnight, but with persistence, proper education, and consistency, it is within reach.

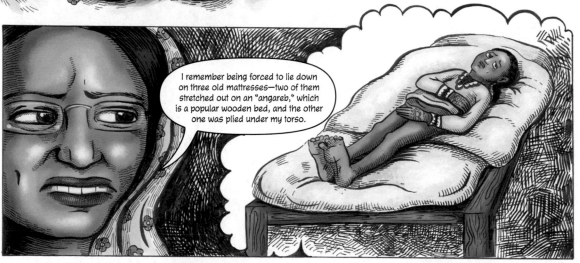

I remember being forced to lie down on three old mattresses—two of them stretched out on an "angareb," which is a popular wooden bed, and the other one was plied under my torso.

My midwife, Hajja Zeinab, sat on a low wooden stool. As she faced my naked body, our eyes met. I tried to escape her firm gaze, but she immediately addressed me with caution.

Now you are a woman. A real woman never cries. Now I will remove this dirt and you will become very clean and a real Muslim.

Later I learned that this belief reveals the depth and core of the atrocity. In Sudan the language plays a major part in making the excision desirable. It is called Tahoura or Tihara, which means purification, thus strongly linking it to religion. I believe this would be the situation for all Muslim communities practicing this ordeal.

125

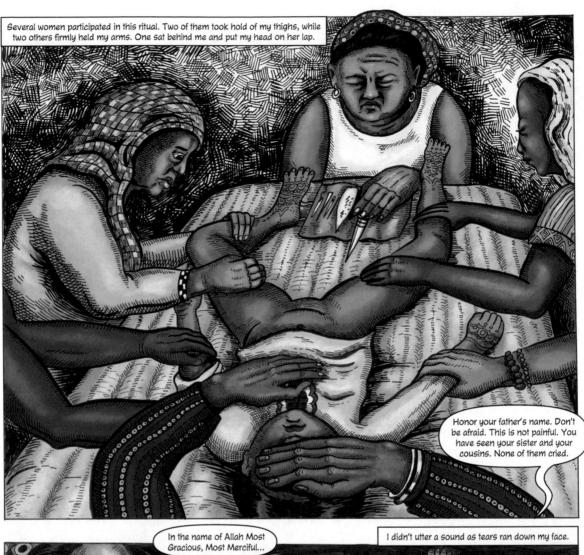

Several women participated in this ritual. Two of them took hold of my thighs, while two others firmly held my arms. One sat behind me and put my head on her lap.

Honor your father's name. Don't be afraid. This is not painful. You have seen your sister and your cousins. None of them cried.

In the name of Allah Most Gracious, Most Merciful...

Open her widely.

I didn't utter a sound as tears ran down my face.

I felt the fingers of Hajja's left hand moving my nudity apart and then a sharp needle pierced my flesh up and down and in the middle.

Oh women, hold her firmly!

AAAAAAAAYYYY!!!

Suddenly, she started cutting. The pain was excruciating. I cried like a mad person. In spite of having her head bent between my thighs I felt as if she was cutting in the middle of my skull. More women were called to help hold me down. Others scolded me for being the only one among the four who had acted cowardly.

Your sister and cousins did not cry. Shame on you!

Does everything look okay?

Coward.

I was anesthetic resistant.

AAAAAAYYYYAAAAHHH

No, no, cut this piece. Yes this one. And remove her clitoris. What is the use of it? And remove the dirt. Do as I tell you.

Grandmother Amna?

Again, Hajja went between my thighs and cut me with the razor. Have I said razor? I am not sure whether it was a razor or a kitchen knife. But I was sure of one ting, she wasn't wearing gloves or covering her head. She wore only her white short dress. She was fat and stout and mowed my flesh with no mercy.

I was only six years old. Too tiny to struggle.

The stitches were the worst part. Nine stitches in all caused me pain and panic whenever I tried to move or urinate.

My sister, two cousins and I (all cut at the same time) were taken outside the excision room and shown the sea. A vision of the sea is believed to serve as a barrier against evil spirits. This evil could be caused by a sudden visit from a relative who might have attended a grievous incident—such as the burial of a dead person—and then surprised us with his presence without informing our mothers to take the necessary precautions. This was believed to cast an evil eye, causing damage to the wound and hindering fast healing.

After the operation, we circumcised girls were well-dressed and ornamented to receive relatives and neighbors who gave us some money.

The celebration seemed like a contradiction. While my sister and cousins and I suffered, the others rejoiced.

For the next seven days, I cried out of pain and suffered urine retention. I couldn't urinate for the first three days following circumcision. Every time I wanted to pass water, I had to bite my lower lip and scream from between my teeth. Since then, the whole process has complicated my life. It is an inconvenience that we bear throughout our lives. We suffer when we get married, we suffer when delivering a child. When we give birth to a child, the operation is repeated: opening, stitching, opening, stitching, retention of urine and so on.

Getting the operation finished was the beginning of an initiation to all woes, instead of womanhood. Nobody told me that it would be a lifetime journey of suffering—during childhood, adolescense, marriage, and childbirth. Six thousand girls are daily cut in Khartoum State alone, more than two million yearly. Growing up, I discovered the dimensions of the problem; FGM is a global ordeal. About one hundred and forty million women are circumcised; the majority of them in Africa (in twenty-eight countries) and the Middle East.

After my FGM ordeal, I fought very hard in order to have my dreams come true. I demanded proper schooling and fought an early arranged marriage and imposed employment. I attained a Bachelor of Art in French and a higher diploma in translation, Arabic to English. I am married with three lovely children. I now work as a freelance journalist, blogger, translator, facilitator, and activist, living abroad and contributing to a large number of media outlets in both Arabic and English. My works are widely quoted by the international and local media. I continue to be passionate about empowering women and helping those marginalized to voice the difficulties they face.

Something must be done to stop this horror!

That was the conviction which didn't leave my mind. In the mid–1980s I began my career of advocacy. I started by speaking up against FGM in my own hometown, merged my advocacy with my journalistic work in the 1990s (for both conventional and digital media), and became a facilitator in 2012.

I started first by targeting victims and executioners. I used to explain to potential victims the damage which would be inflicted on them if they were to accept temptations of having this dangerous operation done to them. I used illustrated books brought from Babiker Badri Scientific Association for Women's Studies. Later, two relatives, a doctor and a religious man, joined me. The three of us targeted all members of the families. Now the number of uncircumcised in my family exceeded 30, including my daughter. Some of these uncircumcised women have graduated from universities, married, and become mothers, thankful for having been spared this horror. Some have also joined in advocacy against FGM.

The image of some of my relatives' sufferings are still vivid in my mind, and nourish my advocacy: Salwa's husband rejected her because she had fistula following a hard late labor. Rugaya's newborn had brain damage that kept him crippled for life.

Three relatives lost their lives during labor.

Two more relatives were divorced because of their reduced sexuality. "How can I live with a cold woman whose vagina is like a leaked irrigation pipe?" asked a man who divorced one of my relatives when asked about reasons for separation.

FGM was responsible for these women's tragedies.

MCFARLAND GRAPHIC NOVELS

Yellow Rose of Texas: The Myth of Emily Morgan.
Written by Douglas Brode; Illustrated by Joe Orsak. 2010

Horrors: Great Stories of Fear and Their Creators.
Written by Rocky Wood; Illustrated by Glenn Chadbourne. 2010

Hutch: Baseball's Fred Hutchinson and a Legacy of Courage.
Written by Mike Shannon; Illustrated by Scott Hannig. 2011

*Hit by Pitch: Ray Chapman, Carl Mays and
the Fatal Fastball.* Molly Lawless. 2012

*Werewolves of Wisconsin and Other American Myths,
Monsters and Ghosts.* Andy Fish. 2012

Witch Hunts: A Graphic History of the Burning Times.
Written by Rocky Wood and Lisa Morton;
Illustrated by Greg Chapman. 2012

*Hardball Legends and Journeymen and Short-Timers: 333
Illustrated Baseball Biographies.* Ronnie Joyner. 2012

The Accidental Candidate: The Rise and Fall of Alvin Greene.
Written by Corey Hutchins and David Axe; Art by Blue Delliquanti. 2012

Virgin Vampires: Or, Once Upon a Time in Transylvania.
Written by Douglas Brode; Illustrated by Joe Orsak. 2012

Great Zombies in History. Edited by Joe Sergi. 2013

Bushers: Ballplayers Drawn from Left Field.
Ed Attanasio and Eric Gouldsberry. 2013

Bonnie and Clyde— The Beginning. Gary Jeffrey. 2014

Dracula's Army: The Dead Travel Fast. Andy Fish. 2014